MIND BENDERS

BRAIN TWISTERS

Author: Paul Hayes

Editor: Dympna Hayes

Art Director: Rick Rowden

Illustrators: Peggy McEwen
              Shane Doyle
              Rick Rowden
              Jodi Shuster
              Sami Suomalainen
              Ashely Lenz
              Arnie Lipsey

Second Printing, 1988
Third Printing, 1992

DURKIN HAYES PUBLISHING LTD.
3312 Mainway, Burlington, Ontario, L7M 1A7, Canada
One Colomba Drive, Niagara Falls, New York 14305, U.S.A.

DUCK HUNTING

There are two ducks in front of two ducks. There are two ducks behind two ducks. There are two ducks between two ducks. How many ducks are there?

WHO DID IT?

Nina, Stefani and Karl had a huge pillow fight. There were feathers all over the room. Their mother came upstairs and found a broken vase. "Who did it?" their mother asked. This is what the children told their mother. Now, one child is lying, one child is telling the truth, and the third child is telling a lie and the truth.

Who broke the vase?

DOWN THE GARDEN PATH

Mr. Mason built four mazes in his garden. Three of the mazes were constructed so that it was possible to pass through every gate exactly once. However, one maze was built so that it was impossible to pass through every gate without passing through one of the gates twice.

Find a path through three of the mazes that passes through every gate exactly once. Find the maze for which this is impossible.

FAMILY TIES

Patrick's sister has one more sister than brothers. How many more sisters than brothers does Patrick have?

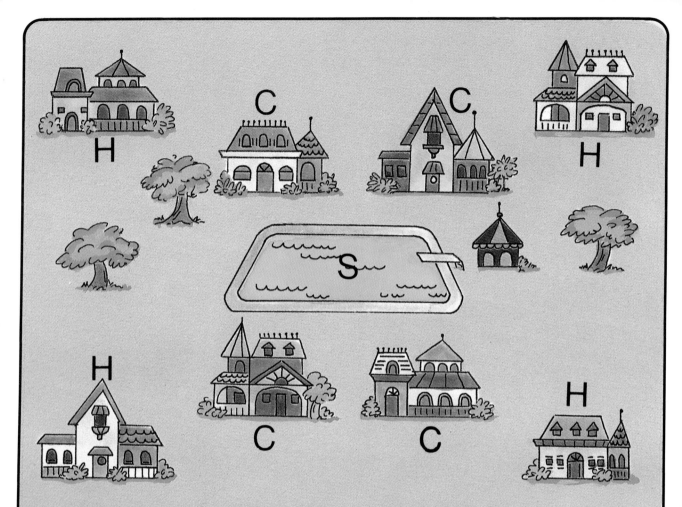

HOUSING PROBLEM

In the drawing above, capital Hs represent houses in which there are no children. The houses represented by C have children living in them. S represents a swimming pool that is shared by the people who live in all eight houses. To protect the children, we must build a fence so that the people in the H houses will be inside the fence and the people in the C houses will have to go through a gate to get to the pool.

How should this fence be built?

LAND HO!

A man sitting on a log at the side of a deep but small lake has been pulling his son across the lake by means of a very long rope attached to a raft on which the son is sitting. As the raft reaches the centre of the lake, the knot holding the rope to the raft gets untied, the rope sinks to the bottom, and the raft is marooned in the middle of the lake.

The raft is too far out for the man to throw the rope to the boy; neither the boy nor the father can swim; the raft cannot be propelled by the boy in any way; and the father has no equipment whatsoever other than that already mentioned.

How does the father bring his son safely to shore under these conditions?

FLOWN THE COOP

My pet bird has flown away and is sitting on a pole in the middle of a farmer's pond. I don't want to go after my bird until I know how deep the pond is, so I asked the farmer. He said, "Well, I musta sunk half that pole in the mud at the bottom of the pond, left 'bout a third sticking outa the mud but underwater, and there's a good half a metre showin' that your pretty bird's asittin' on." Great, I thought. I still don't know how deep the pond is, or do I?

MOBIUS STRIP

Here's a logic puzzle that you can't solve — just enjoy it! You need some paper, a pencil, scissors and tape.

Take a long strip of paper (or stick some short ones end to end), give the strip one twist and tape the ends together. Now, before you go further, think about this: Everything has two sides, right? No matter how thin something is, it will always have a front and a back. Think about it for a minute, then do the next step.

Take a pencil and draw a line down the middle of one side of the loop. On which side did you draw? The only side! That's right! (A little one-dimensional fun!)

Next, cut along your pencil line; go all the way around carefully. You'd expect two loops, right? Not today, because you are playing with a Mobius strip. Some things in the world are special; the Mobius strip is one of them. Now try cutting down the middle of your big loop.

Try some other Mobius tricks. Try making one with two twists, or try cutting from ⅓ of the edge, all the way around. Make up your own Mobius ideas.

There is a wonderful science-fiction short story called *A Subway Named Mobius*. You might enjoy reading it some day.

SWIMMING TEST

The "Dolphins" and "Porpoises" are two swimming clubs at the same level in swim school. They both had to take a test to pass the course. Here are some important points:

1. Some "Dolphins" are almost as good at swimming as the "Porpoises."

2. There are more children in the "Dolphins" class than in the "Porpoises" class.

3. More than half the "Porpoises" passed the swim test.

4. Less than half of all the children didn't pass.

Did any "Dolphins" pass the swim test? Which two of the four points indicate whether or not they passed?

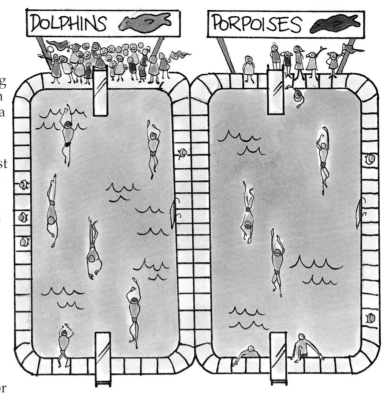

SWEET TOOTH

Susan was making some coffee. When she reached for the cupboard, she knocked over the sugar bowl and at least half a dozen loose sugar cubes fell into her coffee. Moments later she had managed to pluck all the sugar cubes out of the coffee which, incidentally, was no sweeter than before the accident. How did she do it?

RELATIVE RIDDLE

John: "That girl, Joanne, is my niece!"

Marsha: "Yes, but she's not my niece."

Peter: "Is John married?"

Joanne: "No, he is Marsha's brother."

What relative is Joanne to Marsha?

LAUNDRY DAYS

A very neat gentleman wears a clean shirt every day. If he drops off his laundry and picks up the previous week's load every Monday night, how many shirts must he own?

SHAKE-UP

There are four people — or two couples. If they shake hands with each other just once, how many handshakes will take place?

FUNNY FOOD

What food is eaten in the following manner: Throw away the outside, cook the inside; eat the outside, throw away the inside?

SENIOR CITIZEN'S SECRET

Sam Smith, the senior citizen, remembered that he was sent to school when he was 4½ years of age and stayed at that same school for 1/6 of his life. Then he remained in the army for 1/5 of his life, and when he left the army he spent ¼ of his life as a baker. At present he has already spent ⅓ of his life in retirement. How old is Sam Smith?

COOCOOLOOKOO CASH

In CooCooLooKooland, pure gold coins are used instead of paper money, and the coins are valued in accordance with their weight.

A $20 gold coin weighs twice as much as a $10 gold coin.

If you visited CooCooLooKooland and someone offered you a 5 kg bag of $20 coins or a 7 kg bag of $10 coins, which should you take?

HEADS UP

A coin with "heads up" is rolled around another coin to the final position shown.

Which of these shows what the coin looks like in the final position?

LUCKY 28

Twenty-eight cents are placed on the table. Each player in turn picks up one, two or three cents from the pile. The player who picks up the last cent is the winner. Here is a strategy that always wins!

Let whoever you're playing with go first, then make sure that whatever number he picks up, you pick up enough to make a total of four.(If he takes one, take three; he takes two, take two; he takes three, take one.)

DRAGGING --- A RACE

As an entertaining change of pace, a race track operator decided to have a "build the slowest car race" between the regular races one weekend. However, the plan seemed to have failed when, fifteen minutes after the race had started, only two of the eleven cars entered had even crossed the starting line. The judges were just about to call it off for fear the fans would get bored and leave when someone had a bright idea. Ten minutes after the contest had been restarted, an entertaining race followed and the crowd cheered the winner as the last car crossed the finish line at its maximum speed of 5 km/h. How had they solved the problem?

SPLITTING BULL

Farmer: "I leave all 17 bulls to my 3 children to divide as follows: Linda gets one-half of the bulls, Bill gets one-third, and Fred gets one-ninth."

Linda: "That means I get 8½ bulls!"

Bill: "I get 5⅔ bulls!"

Fred: "I get 1-8/9 bulls!"

Linda: "Oh my goodness! How will we divide the bulls without splitting any?"

A neighboring farmer came along leading a bull. He quickly solved their problem and then he and his bull went merrily on their way! Can you work out how he did it?

WINDOW WASHERS

Window cleaners sometimes work in teams, with one man washing insides only while the other does the outsides. On a particular day, one man came to work early and had already washed four insides when his partner arrived and reminded him that he was supposed to be the "outside" man that day. The latecomer then took over the work on the insides, while the early bird started on the outsides. When the inside man completed all the remaining insides, he helped the outside man finish by washing eight outsides.

If we consider an inside or an outside to be one window, who washed more windows that day, and how many more did he wash?

THE AGE-OLD PROBLEM

What is the answer to
Professor Hoffnagel's question?

WHAT ARE THEY?

These are usually found in any hardware store. Every home has at least one. You can buy one for $.25, 12 for $.50, 120 for $.75 and 1,200 for $1.00. What are they?

BUNNY BURROW

In a certain rabbit family, every little girl rabbit has the same number of brothers as she has sisters, and each boy rabbit has twice as many sisters as he has brothers.

How many boys are there, and how many girls are there?

RUN, JOHNNY, RUN!

A man was walking down a lonely country road. Neither the moon nor the stars were out. The man did not have a flashlight, nor a reflector of any kind. He did not have any light-coloured clothing. From behind, a car comes speeding down the road without any headlights on, headed directly toward the man who was walking in the centre of the road.

The walking man made no sounds, movements, or any effort to move from the road to let the driver know he was there, yet the driver of the car knew the man was there and stopped before he hit him. Why?

TOOTHPICK TRICK

Can you take away six toothpicks and end up with ten?

THE TRADING POST

Read this cartoon carefully, then answer this question. Who is in the portrait?

THAT'S A FINE PAINTING YOU HAVE UP THERE ON YOUR WALL, PETE... IS IT A RELATIVE OF YOURS?

WELL...BROTHERS AND SISTERS I HAVE NONE...BUT THAT MAN'S FATHER IS MY FATHER'S SON.

SALT

DANNY'S DESTINATION

All the trains from Union Station go to Lennox. From Lennox, some go to Peterston, others to Jacksonville and then to Midtown; others to Greenfield and on to Marley. The fare is $3.00 to Peterston, Midtown or Marley; elsewhere — $2.00.

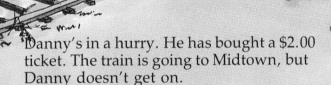

Danny's in a hurry. He has bought a $2.00 ticket. The train is going to Midtown, but Danny doesn't get on.

What is Danny's destination?

JACKSONVILLE

PETERSTON ★

MIDTOWN

GREENFIELD

MARLEY STATION

17

THE WISEST IN THE LAND

The king needed a new chief advisor. He took all his advisors and wise men to a large room that had a very large carpet in the middle and in the middle of the carpet was a big bag of gold. The king proclaimed "Whoever can pick up this bag of gold while keeping his feet on the tile floor and using no tools, shall be my right-hand advisor. That person shall be acclaimed the wisest in the land and receive many privileges as well as this heavy bag of gold."

Days later the wise men were mad with frustration, but that was nothing compared to how they felt when the court jester walked in and walked out moments later with the bag of gold, the wisest man in the kingdom.

How did he do it?

SS UNSINKABLE

Captain Penworthy was standing at the stern of the SS Unsinkable, pondering a question posed to him by a crew member. "Captain," the crew member said, "it's low tide now and six rungs of our boarding ladder are underwater. I've measured and the rungs are twenty-three centimetres apart. The tide rises fast around here — half a metre per hour, in fact. I'm worried, Captain. How many rungs of the ladder will be underwater three hours from now?"

FILL 'ER UP

Three glasses are full of ice-cold soda; three are empty. They are arranged like this:

How would you rearrange them like this:

In the least number of moves?

CAREFUL CROSSING

A farmer must transport a dog, a duck and a bag of corn from one side of a river to the other. His tiny boat is large enough to take only one of his possessions across at one time. If he leaves the dog alone with the duck, the dog will gobble up the duck. If he leaves the duck alone with the corn, the duck will gobble up the corn. What is the least number of trips the farmer can take to manage safely?

WHO FLIPPED OUT?

Vampires don't make reflections in a mirror. Some of these letters are not vampires because they have been reflected. Can you tell which ones?

Be careful! Some are just turned, not flipped.

See if you can find all seven of them.

THE PRISONERS' PROBLEM

Three prisoners were brought before the king. "Each of you ," said the king, "will be given five coloured balls and five black balls that you may put into two bowls in any way you please. You will then be blindfolded and your two bowls moved around.

You must select a ball from one of the bowls. If it is coloured, you will be freed. If it is black, you will die."

Here's a picture of how the prisoners distributed their 10 balls.

Which man has the
a) greatest chance of choosing a coloured ball?

b) least chance of choosing a coloured ball?

ALL SLIPPED UP

Sam, the silly sailor, hasn't kept his boat very neat. Now he has to straighten things up, starting by untangling the ropes. Which of the knots in the rope will come out if Sam pulls the rope tight?

WHAT IS IT?

The man who made it, couldn't use it.
The man who bought it, didn't
need it.
The man who got it, didn't know it.
What was it?

SAY WHAT?

There were three secret groups in town
and these friends — Derek, Cyril and
R.D. — had each joined one. The groups
were: The W.L.F.F.A. (We Lie For Fun
Always), the Noble Knights (who always
told the truth) and the Yin Yangs (who
sometimes told the truth, sometimes lied).

Cathy, a friend of all three, was trying to
find out which group each had joined.
She knew for sure that at least one was in

the Noble Knights. These were secret
groups, so each person would only hint
about the groups they joined.

Could Cathy work it out? They all seemed
so sure of themselves. Can you work it out?
Try using the solution method from "Who
Did It?" on page 2.

R.D. said, "We all joined
the same group and are
now proud agents of the
W.L.F.F.A."

To which Cyril replied, "No!
Only one of us belongs to a
different group, and that
one is a W.L.F.F.A. agent."

And Derek said, "We all
joined different groups and
R.D. is a W.L.F.F.A. agent."

CLIP TRICK

Here's an interesting puzzle about yourself.

1. Unfold a paper clip into a "V" shape. Try to make the "legs" the same length.

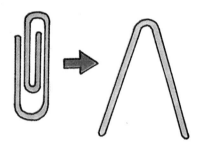

2. Hang it over a pencil and hold the pencil straight so that both "legs" of the paper clip just touch the tabletop or a piece of paper laying flat on a tabletop.

3. Try not to let the paper clip move.

Why, when you try hard to hold still, does the paper clip move faster?

PLAYING CARDS

Three playing cards are in a row. A diamond is on the left of a spade (but not necessarily next to it). An eight is on the right of a king. A ten is on the left of a heart. A heart is on the left of a spade.

What are the three playing cards?

FANTASTIC PHYSICAL FEATS

Reading books shouldn't be just exercising your eyes — get up and try these.

1. Standing with your heels against the wall, try to bend over and touch the ground without bending your knees.

2. Stand shoulders, heels and back against the wall — jump!

3. Now, try this. Put all your knuckles together and touch your ring fingers together. Have a friend put a coin between your two fingers. Now, without sliding your fingers apart and still holding your knuckles together, try to drop the coin!

Frustrated? Just one more physical puzzle. Kiss your elbow! Nice try!

PLANE TO MALAGA

Patrick and his friends were flying from Toronto, Canada, to Malaga, Spain, for a holiday. There were many people going back and forth between these two cities, so there was a plane leaving from Malaga to Toronto every hour, and one from Toronto to Malaga every hour.

Now, not counting the plane that lands from Malaga in Toronto as they take off, or the one that leaves Malaga as they land, how many planes flying from Malaga to Toronto will Patrick and his friends pass on their seven-hour flight? (It takes seven hours to fly from Toronto to Malaga, and from Malaga to Toronto also takes seven hours, travelling at the same speed.)

Hint — it's not 6 or 7!

PING PONG PARTY

Mary, her dad, her husband Gord, and Mary and Gord's daughter, Jessica, were playing doubles ping pong. After the game, when recounting a funny moment, one of the players described the situation.

"I was directly across the net from the server's daughter. My partner (on the same side of the net as myself) was directly across the net from the receiver's daughter. The server (in keeping with the rules) was diagonally across the net from the receiver."

The question is — Who spoke and what were the teams? Try drawing a diagram and filling in names, starting with who you think is speaking. If it doesn't work, try it with someone else speaking.

THE EIGHT BRIDGES OF EDGARTOWN

This picture shows the eight bridges of Edgartown. Many people of Edgartown have tried with great difficulty to cross each bridge exactly once and without missing any of the bridges.

Starting at the red bridge on the left-hand side of the page, see if you can cross all the bridges once only and end at the centre island where the kids are flying a kite. Good luck! Remember not to ruin your book by writing in it. Draw a little diagram on a piece of paper instead.

PAGE 2
DUCK HUNTING
There are 4 ducks in a row
2 in front of 2
2 behind 2
2 between 2

LOOK-ALIKES
They are triplets; the other brother's not there.

WHO DID IT?
Hint - Try assuming one of them did and see if the requirements that one lied, one told the truth, and one lied and told the truth are met.
Answer-
Stefani did it because it is the only case that makes for the right combination of true/false answers.

PAGE 3
DOWN THE GARDEN PATH

No path can be made in this garden without going through at least one gateway twice.

FAMILY TIES
Patrick has 3 more sisters than brothers.

Imagine there were five sisters and three brothers. If one of the sisters counted, she'd see herself as having 4 sisters and 3 brothers or one more sister than she has brothers. If one of the brothers counted, he'd see himself as having 2 brothers and 5 sisters or 3 more sisters than brothers.

PAGE 4
HOUSING PROBLEM

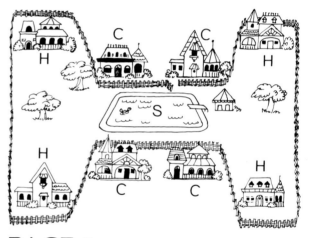

PAGE 5
LAND HO!
The father ties the very long rope to a tree and then walks around the end of the lake and around the other side, so the rope is stretched across the lake, and the son can grab it.

PAGE 6
FLOWN THE COOP
½ the pole is in the mud, ⅓ is underwater and half a metre is showing.

1/2 + 1/3 + half a metre = length of the pole
Since 1/2 = 3/6 and 1/3 = 2/6 then
3/6 + 2/6 + half a metre = length of the pole
3/6 + 2/6 = 5/6, so there's 1/6 left out of the water,
so half a metre = 1/6 of the pole.
The pole is 3 metres tall, 1/3 is underwater but out of the ground.
1/3 of 3 metres is 1 metre. So, he'll have to ask the farmer to wade in and grab the bird.

PAGE 7
SWIMMING TEST
Yes, some Dolphins must have passed the test.
Why? Points 2 and 4 tell you. There are more Dolphins than Porpoises, and more than half the children passed. If only Porpoises had passed, it would be less than half the kids.

SWEET TOOTH
It was the dry coffee grounds; she hadn't made the coffee yet.

PAGE 8
RELATIVE RIDDLE
Joanne is Marsha's daughter.

LAUNDRY DAYS
15 shirts
He must pick up 7 to get him through each week, so he must drop off 7 each week, plus the one he is wearing when he goes to the cleaners is 15.

PAGE 9
SHAKE-UP
6 handshakes must take place.

FUNNY FOOD
Corn on the cob

SENIOR CITIZEN'S SECRET
He is 90 years old

$4\frac{1}{2}$ years + 1/6 + 1/5 + ¼ + ⅓ = his age

$4\frac{1}{2}$ years + 10/60 + 12/60 + 15/60 + 20/60 = his age

$4\frac{1}{2}$ years + 57/60 = his age

$4\frac{1}{2}$ years = his age − 57/60

$4\frac{1}{2}$ years = 3/60 of his age

$1\frac{1}{2}$ years = 1/60 his age

$1\frac{1}{2} \times 60$ = his age

90 = his age

PAGE 10
COOCOOLOOKOO CASH
The 7 kg bag!
Since the coins are valued by weight and a $20 coin weighs twice as much as a $10 coin, one $20 coin and two $10 coins would weigh the same. The correct answer is to take the heavier bag; it would be worth more.

HEADS UP
Position 2. Try it; don't let the coin spin.

LUCKY 27
You will always win!

If your opponent wishes to go second, try to pick up these cents: the 7th, 11th, 15th, 19th, and especially the 23rd.

PAGE 11
DRAGGING A RACE

They had each driver drive someone else's car. That way they'd make sure each car went as fast as it could so it would cross the finish line sooner and lose. The last car across the line would truly be the slowest!

SPLITTING BULL

The neighbor added his bull, gave half the bulls to Linda (9), one-third to Bill (6) and one-ninth to Fred (2). This left the one he originally gave them, so he kept it!

PAGE 12
WINDOW WASHERS

The latecomer washed 8 more windows. Imagine there were 100 windows on the building. That's 200 insides and outsides in total.

PAGE 13
THE AGE OLD PROBLEM

Brenda is the oldest, then Betty, then Barbara, then Bunny!

WHAT ARE THEY?

House numbers, at 25 cents per digit.

PAGE 14
BUNNY BURROW

There are 4 girl rabbits and 3 boy rabbits.

RUN, JOHNNY, RUN!

It was daytime!

PAGE 15
TOOTHPICK TRICK

THE TRADING POST

It's Pete's son.

PAGE 16
DANNY'S DESTINATION

A $3.00 ticket gets you to Peterston, Midtown or Marley. So, a $2.00 ticket takes you to Lennox, Greenfield or Jacksonville. Since the train to Midtown goes through Lennox, to Jacksonville, and then to Midtown, if Danny doesn't get on it, he must be going to Greenfield.

PAGE 18
THE WISEST IN THE LAND

He rolled up the carpet.

PAGE 19
SS UNSINKABLE

As Capt. Penworthy flung the crew member overboard, he yelled after him, "6, you fool, the boat floats, doesn't she?"

FILL'ER UP

One move. Pick up the 5th glass, pour it into the 2nd and set it back down.

CAREFUL CROSSING

1. First he takes the duck over.
2. Then he takes the dog over, but brings the duck back.
3. Then he takes the corn over.
4. Then he takes the duck!

PAGE 20

PAGE 21

THE PRISONERS' PROBLEM

Prisoner 102 has the worst chances - One dish, he dies; the other, he has a 5 in 9 chance to live.
Prisoner 101 has slightly better odds - One dish, he lives; one dish, he dies.
Prisoner 103 has the best chances - One dish, he lives; the other he has a 4/9 chance.

PAGE 22

ALL SLIPPED UP

Knots #1 and #3 will come undone. In other words, "They're not knots!"

PAGE 23

WHAT IS IT?

A coffin.

SAY WHAT?

R.D. - W.L.F.F.A.
Cyril - Yin Yang
Derek - Noble Knights

PAGE 24

CLIP TRICK

When you grip something, your muscle cells actually flex and unflex constantly. The tighter you grip, the faster they flex. It's this flexing that causes the paper clip to move. The harder the grip, the faster it moves!

PLAYING CARDS

Left to right
10 of diamonds, King of hearts, 8 of spades

PAGE 25
PLANE TO MALAGA

13 planes will be passed by Patrick's plane!

1. As Patrick's plane leaves, one plane from Malaga lands. Don't count it!

2. As Patrick's plane leaves, there are 6 planes in the air travelling from Malaga to Toronto, one hour apart. Patrick's plane will pass these, so count them.

3. As Patrick's plane leaves Toronto, one plane is leaving Malaga. Count this one; they'll pass it.

4. Patrick's plane will be flying for 7 hours, so 7 planes leave Malaga. Patrick's plane will pass 6 of these in flight. The last one takes off just as Patrick lands, so don't count it. That means count 6 more planes.

PAGE 26
PING PONG PARTY

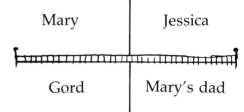

Mary   Jessica

Gord   Mary's dad

Mary's dad did the talking. They were positioned as in the diagram.

Mary serves to her dad.

PAGE 27
THE EIGHT BRIDGES OF EDGARTOWN

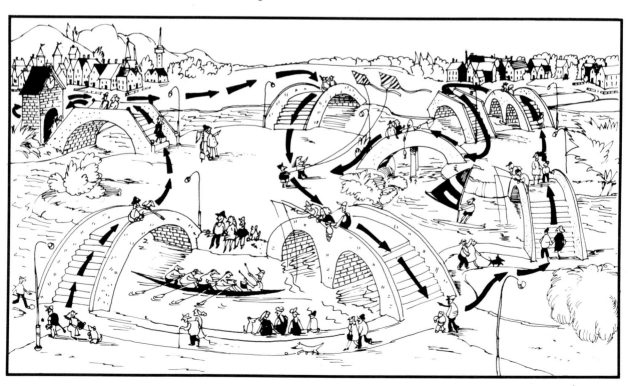